That
Man

Annie Billups

sundown books

New Readers Press ● Syracuse, New York

To Anna Mae and Herman Ripley
and Margaret Ray
who know where Florida Beach really is

ISBN 0-88336-766-1

©1990

New Readers Press
Publishing Division of Laubach Literacy International
Box 131, Syracuse, New York 13210

Printed in the United States of America

Edited by Maria A. Collis
Illustrations by Fred Del Guidice
Cover design by Chris Steenwerth
Cover illustration by Fred Del Guidice

9 8 7 6 5 4 3 2

Table of Contents

Chapter 1

A Date

"You're acting like a silly, old fool!" Flora said. She wrinkled her nose as though something smelled bad.

Flora stood there ramrod-straight in the bathroom doorway, watching Belle get ready. Flora's dark blue dress was so stiffly starched that it seemed to disapprove, too.

Belle went on fixing her hair. She was used to her sister, Flora. Flora was seven years older than Belle, and she never let Belle forget it. Even now, with both of them in their sixties, Flora acted as if she knew better than Belle—about everything. That included men, even though neither sister had ever married.

"Did you hear me?" Flora said, raising her voice. "I said, you're acting like a fool!"

"Um," was Belle's only answer. Then, she yelped, "Ouch!" Her hot curling iron had brushed against her ear. She stuck her finger in her mouth, then touched the sore spot. She didn't like to admit that Flora had upset her with her remarks. After all, why shouldn't Belle want to look nice when Judd took her to the movies?

Belle thought about Judd. So what if he wasn't rich and was a little hard of hearing? He was a very nice man, tall and quiet and very polite.

Belle had secretly liked him for a long time. She thought his thick, gray hair was real handsome. Judd was a widower who had retired several years ago. Now, he kept busy doing odd jobs for people.

Judd, like Belle and Flora, had always lived in the town of Little Creek, in New York State. The town wasn't much, but it was nice and quiet. There were just a few small stores, a diner, a movie theater, and two churches. All around the town were farms.

Now and then, Judd would take one of the single ladies to a movie or to the diner. The Palace Cinema and the Dew-Drop-In Diner were about the only places in town to take anyone. The young folks who were dating went over to Bristol City, where there was more excitement.

But Belle was excited. This was the third time Judd had asked her out!

She put a final touch of curl to the ends of her faded, blonde hair. The ends always slipped out of the knot she made on top of her head. Curling them made her look younger, she thought. Sort of perky.

"There," she said. "That will have to do."

Just then, the doorbell rang, and Flora hurried away to answer it. Flora always liked to answer the doorbell and the telephone. It was her way of telling people that she was the boss of the household.

Belle hurried to get downstairs before Flora could start in on Judd. But she was too late. Flora was already in full swing.

"Why, you should be ashamed of yourself!" Flora's voice was full of scorn. "Just look at you, Judd Hagadorn. I know you're color-blind, but you've got on green pants and a blue jacket. And you're wearing one brown shoe and one black one! If you don't beat all!"

Judd just stood there quietly, in the middle of the room.

Flora went on. "Why in the world a man your age wants to go around taking women out beats me! You should have better things to do with your time and money. And when you *do* go out, you show up looking half-witted! Don't you ever look in the mirror?"

"Good evening, Judd!" Belle said, hurrying into the living room. "I see you're right on time! I like a man who's punctual!"

Judd turned and faced Belle. At first, there was a confused look on his face. Then, he broke into a smile.

"Oh, just a minute, Belle," he said. He put his hand to his ear for a moment. Then, he nodded his head, smiling. "Would you mind repeating what you just said? I had to turn my hearing aid back on."

Flora looked mad enough to spit when she found out Judd hadn't heard a word she said. But Belle just grabbed her coat, hooked her arm through Judd's, and hurried him out the door. No sense in letting Flora get started again.

Chapter 2

A Lucky Drawing

After they had climbed into his old Chevy, Judd asked, "Still feel like going to the movies, Belle?"

"Yes," she said. "I'm looking forward to it."

They didn't talk much on the way. Judd liked to think about his driving when he was driving. Belle thought that was a good trait for a man to have.

At the theater, there were quite a few people in line for tickets. When they got their tickets, Judd and Belle went into the dark theater. They managed to find two seats on the aisle. Judd liked to sit next to the aisle so he could stretch his legs out.

"This is nice," Belle said, inching closer to him. "It's so cozy to watch a movie with a friend."

Just then, the lights dimmed, and the movie started.

It was a pretty good movie. It was about a pair of detectives in Beverly Hills and the things that happened to them.

"How exciting their lives must be," Belle said to Judd. He didn't hear her, though, and she didn't want to say it any louder.

When intermission came, a big sign flashed on the screen saying that the Palace Cinema was having a big contest.

"Look at that!" Belle said, pointing to the words on the screen. "The Palace is giving away a pair of train tickets to Florida!"

Judd looked at her and smiled. "I've always wanted to go to Florida," he said shyly. "My boy lives down in Florida Beach. He keeps asking me to come down, but it costs a lot of money to take a trip like that."

"I know," Belle agreed. "I was there once, years and years ago. I remember how excited I was to see so much sun in the winter!"

The words on the screen explained that everybody who bought a giant-size box of popcorn would be entered in the contest. On the inside of each popcorn box, there was a number. After the movie, there would be a drawing. Some lucky person whose number was picked would win two round-trip train tickets to Florida.

"Imagine that!" breathed Belle. "Wouldn't it be wonderful?"

"You like popcorn?" Judd asked.

"Oh, yes!" Belle burst out. "I love it!"

"Be right back," Judd said. He got up and headed towards the refreshment stand in the lobby.

A lot of people were hurrying to buy popcorn, so it was a while before Judd came back. In each hand he held the biggest box of popcorn Belle had ever seen. She had to reach over and hold down his seat because Judd's hands were so full. He smiled his thanks and sat down. Then, he handed her a box of popcorn.

Belle and Judd started chewing their way through the huge amounts of popcorn. It took them almost through the second half of the movie to finish it all.

As soon as the movie ended, a big sign came on the screen again. "Last chance to buy popcorn and enter the contest," it said. A lot of people hurried back to get another box. Belle and Judd waited patiently. Not one person had left the Palace.

"I guess everyone wants to win," Belle said.

"Looks that way," Judd agreed.

Just then, all the lights in the theater came on. A man and woman were standing on the stage at the front. The woman was holding a big cardboard box filled with little pieces of paper. The man was holding a microphone. He seemed to be fussing with it.

Finally, there was a screechy noise on the loudspeaker. Then, a crackly voice said, "All right, everyone. I'm Mr. Zebhart, and this is my wife. We're the owners of the Palace, and we're here to choose the winner of the tickets to Florida. Get your popcorn boxes ready, so you can read the numbers in 'em. We're going to do the drawing right now!"

Belle had memorized her number, 4240. Even so, she tipped up the box and looked at it again.

"Are you ready?" Mr. Zebhart's voice crackled over the speaker. Then, he reached over and took a slip of paper out of Mrs. Zebhart's box. Everyone watched as he unfolded the slip of paper. He paused a moment to make it seem more exciting. Then, he showed the number to Mrs. Zebhart.

"The winning number is four, two, four, zero!" Mr. Zebhart said. "Did you all hear me? The winning number is forty-two forty! Who's the lucky winner? Who gets the free tickets to Florida?"

Belle looked around at all the people. Any minute now, someone would let out a happy yell and jump up, all excited. She strained her eyes trying to see all the people at once.

Then, it hit her.

"I won!" she cried, throwing her arms around Judd's neck in excitement. "I won, Judd. I won the tickets to Florida!"

"You did?" Judd asked, not daring to believe it. But, when Belle tipped up her box so he could see her number, his face broke into a maze of happy wrinkles. "You really did!" he cried.

Judd hurried to his feet, pulling Belle with him. She started waving her empty popcorn box in the air as they hurried down the aisle. She was laughing to beat all.

Judd was so excited that he shouted, "She won it! She won it!"

Mr. Zebhart helped Belle up onto the stage and reached for her box. After Belle's number had been checked, Mrs. Zebhart handed her an envelope. Then, Mr. and Mrs. Zebhart took turns shaking Belle's hand. There was a lot of clapping and whistling. Just then, another man came up on the stage with a camera and took a picture of Belle standing with the Zebharts. The picture was for the local paper.

When it was all over, Belle got down off the stage and started towards the back of the theater with Judd. Belle clutched the envelope in her hand. None of it seemed real to her.

"Want to stop for a late hamburger?" Judd asked. "Seems we ought to do something special."

"Why, I'd like that," Belle answered. She didn't want this wonderful evening to end.

At the diner, waiting for their food, Belle read the words on the envelope for about the 10th time.

"These tickets are good until December thirty-first. When you decide on the date you wish to use them, call the Amtrak office. Your dated tickets will be sent right to your home."

Just as the waitress brought their order, an idea flashed into Belle's mind.

"Judd, I only won these tickets because you bought me that popcorn," Belle said. "So, the fair thing to do is share the prize with you."

Judd looked at her, puzzled.

"I'm asking if you'd like to go to Florida with me," Belle said. She surprised herself by daring to suggest such a thing. She could just picture how Flora would react!

"After all, lots of men and women travel together these days," Belle went on. "It's perfectly all right. And I think it would be real nice if you got to see your son."

Judd looked surprised for a minute. Then, his face lit up like an early sunrise. "I'll do it!" he said. "By golly, I'll do it!"

Chapter 3

Off to Florida!

When Belle won the contest, it was March. There was still snow on the ground in Little Creek. People walked around in heavy coats and boots or rubbers, longing for spring. All except Belle and Judd, that is. For the next few weeks, they were busy making plans for their trip to Florida. Belle pulled out her best summer dresses and skirts.

Flora made catty little remarks every chance she got. But, when she saw Belle getting ready to pack a bathing suit, she spoke her mind straight out.

"It's just not decent!" Flora said. "No proper woman takes a trip with a man she's not married or engaged to!" Then, she sniffed loudly and walked away very fast, her shoes clicking on the floor.

But, in spite of Flora, the plans went ahead. Finally, it was time to leave. When Judd came for Belle, she thought he looked quite handsome in his new gray slacks and sweater. He picked Belle up early. She was excited and just wanted to sit in the Bristol City station and watch the people. Judd was really more excited than he let on, too.

In the station, Belle made comments to Judd about all the people waiting for trains. "I wonder if they're going to Florida, too?" Belle said. She pointed to an older couple pushing a cart loaded with heavy suitcases. "I'll just bet they are!" she said, sounding happy.

Then, she noticed a man sitting in the corner of the station all by himself. Something about him didn't seem right to her. She wasn't sure what it was but, somehow, she felt uneasy as she turned away. She began to watch an older woman trying to keep a busy little boy in tow. Every time the woman got the little boy settled on her lap, he wiggled off and scooted away.

"I'll just bet she's his grandma," Belle said. As she turned back to look for the little boy again, she had the creepy feeling that she was being watched. She looked again at the man sitting in the corner. He seemed to be reading a newspaper. Still, she had a funny feeling about him. She turned away.

Judd looked at his watch. "Shouldn't be too much longer, Belle," he said.

"Good!" she said. "I can hardly wait!" She turned to look again at the man in the corner. As though he knew she was looking at him, he raised his eyes and looked directly at her. She had never seen such cold, dark eyes in all her life! A chill went up her back, and she shivered.

"What's the matter, Belle? You catching a cold?" Judd asked.

"No, no. It's just that man over there."

"What man?" Judd asked, looking around.

Belle motioned quickly. "That man in the corner. There's something about him that gives me the creeps."

Judd looked over towards the corner and saw a man busy reading his newspaper. Judd looked at Belle for a moment, wondering. He sure hoped she wasn't going to turn out to be one of those nervous types. She had always seemed so full of common sense before.

"You must be imagining things," he said. "The man's just minding his own business."

Just then, the train came, and they forgot about the man in the flurry of getting aboard.

When they were safely on board and had found seats, Belle sighed and settled back. She watched as Judd stowed the last of their baggage on the rack overhead. He sat down beside her and looked around.

"We're on our way at last!" she said.

The six-hour trip to New York passed quickly. Belle had brought sandwiches, and Judd bought them each a cola. They enjoyed eating while they watched the countryside flash by. The hours passed as fast as the landscape.

"Uh-oh," said Judd, leaning to look out the window. "We're coming into New York City. I'm a little worried about getting that shuttle over to Penn Station."

"Well, the conductor said somebody from the railroad would be there to meet us," Belle told him. She was worried about having to change trains and train stations, too.

The train finally came to a stop in Grand Central Station. People jammed the aisles, grabbing their things from the luggage rack. Just then, the lights went out!

"Oh, bullets!" Judd yelled, as one of the bags slid down off the rack and bumped his shoulder.

"Are you all right?" Belle asked, worried.

"Everyone taking the train through to Florida come this way!" The conductor's voice came from outside on the station platform.

"Oh, hurry, Judd. Hurry!" Belle urged.

"It's OK, Belle. You just take these two duffel bags, and I'll bring the big ones," he said.

Tugging and pushing, they squeezed their way out of the train onto the platform.

"There he is, Belle!" Judd cried. "Come on!" He hurried off, doing his best to follow the conductor.

"Wait, wait for me!" Belle yelled as someone bumped into her and sent all her luggage tumbling.

There was a rush of people hurrying by. Belle stopped to try and pick up her luggage before it was lost. Just as she bent to pick up her duffel bag, she saw the suspicious man she had seen back in the train station.

"Why, I'll bet he's the one who pushed me!" she said to herself. But she was too busy trying to catch up to Judd to think any more about it.

Suddenly, the crowd stopped pushing its way forward and seemed to be waiting for something.

"Right this way to the shuttle!" came the conductor's voice. "This way!" he sang out, and the crowd surged forward again.

A bus stood waiting. The bus driver took their baggage and hurried Belle onto the bus.

She found Judd already on the bus. He had saved a seat for her.

"Oh, thank goodness!" she said, sinking into the seat beside him. "You'll never believe what happened to me!"

But she never got to tell him, because the conductor told them all to listen to some important announcements. Then, the bus began to move and, in no time, they were at Penn Station. And the shoving and tugging began all over again.

A nice, older redcap seemed to take pity on Belle and Judd.

"For just a dollar a bag I'll get you folks right on the train to Florida," he said.

Judd didn't stop to think about it. He dug four dollars out of his wallet and gave it to the redcap. Belle and Judd followed the redcap through the gate, down to the big empty train. A man opened the door and let them in, and the redcap put their bags up in the luggage rack.

"Told you I'd get you right in," the redcap said with a grin. Then, he hurried off.

A big group of boys and girls got on the train. They were laughing and shoving each other.

A worried-looking woman with the group leaned over as they passed Belle's seat.

"We're taking our eighth grade class to Washington to see the sights," she said with a sigh. "I wonder if I'll live through it."

Belle and Judd laughed and watched the group's progress through the car.

"They don't seem to have much luggage," Judd said. "But did you ever see anyone carrying so many boxes of fried chicken and pizza?"

"They came well prepared," Belle laughed. "Oh, we're moving!" she said, looking out the window to see the platform sliding by. Just then, she saw the suspicious man hurrying to catch the train.

"He's going to be on this train, Judd," she said, grabbing Judd's arm to get his attention.

"Who is?" Judd asked.

"Why, *him!* You know, that man. The man I saw in the station at Bristol City. I pointed him out to you. He's the one who knocked the suitcases out of my hands, too. I'm sure of it," she insisted.

Judd didn't seem to hear her. "Look, Belle," he said, pointing. "We've just left the station. Now, we're on the best part of the trip."

Belle was annoyed that Judd had ignored what she said. But she just sat quietly next to him and watched as the houses and towns seemed to flow by. They watched until it began to grow dark.

22

Chapter 4

The Wrong Bag

When it was too dark to see much out the window, Belle began to study the people in their car. There were all kinds. Some of them seemed to be in family groups, but others were by themselves.

"I wonder how many of them are going all the way to Florida," Belle said.

"No way of knowing," Judd answered. "I think I'll read," he said. He stood up to get a book out of his small suitcase and sat down with a sigh of satisfaction. "Imagine," he said to Belle, smiling, "I'm going to read my way from New York through New Jersey. I'll read all the way to Philadelphia!"

Belle laughed happily. "Oh, no, Judd. We get to Philadelphia *before* we get to New Jersey."

Judd looked at her. "Belle, what's wrong with your geography? We go through New Jersey first."

"No, we don't, Judd," she said. "Tell you what. If you'll reach down my duffel bag, I'll hunt out that big map I packed and *show* you!"

"Bet you the cost of supper you're wrong!" Judd said with a roguish gleam in his eye.

"I'll bet you I'm not!" Belle snapped back.

Judd stood up and pulled Belle's duffel bag off the rack. He laid it in her lap and sat down to wait.

Belle unzipped the duffel bag. Then, her face got a funny expression on it.

"Why, Judd, this isn't my bag!"

"Of course it's your bag. I put it up there on the shelf myself," Judd said.

"I know I brought a duffel bag, Judd. But this isn't it! This one's green, and mine is blue!"

"Are you sure?" Judd asked, leaning over to see. "It sure looks like yours!"

"Oh, Judd," she said more gently. "You're color-blind. You can't tell the difference between green and blue. But look inside. See? These aren't my things at all!"

Belle pointed at the men's shaving things in the top of the duffel.

"But I don't see—," Judd began.

"There's the conductor," Belle cried. "Call him over here, Judd!"

When the conductor came, Belle told him about the mix-up with her luggage.

The conductor listened patiently. "What is it you want me to do, ma'am?"

"Why, search the train and find my bag!" Belle said. "I don't know whose this is." She pointed to the bag in her lap. "But it certainly isn't mine!"

"I can't do that, ma'am—," the conductor started to say.

"Of course you can!" Belle broke in. "Isn't that the sort of thing you're here for?"

The conductor looked as if he wished he were somewhere else.

"I'm sorry, ma'am. But I can't do that. I can announce it on the loudspeaker, though." When Belle started to shake her head in protest, he went on. "You see, ma'am, there are seven coach cars and six sleepers, and I'm only assigned to *this* car. I don't belong all over the train."

Belle was beginning to look quite angry.

"Don't worry," the conductor said. "We'll get it all straightened out before you get to Florida."

Then, he scurried off down the aisle.

Belle sat up very straight and squared her shoulders. "All right, then. I'll do it myself!"

"What are you going to do?" Judd asked.

"I'm going to take care of this myself!" Belle said. And, without another word, she popped up out of her seat and started down the aisle. Before Judd could figure out what to do, Belle had disappeared from sight.

At the end of the car was a heavy door that led to the next car. Belle opened the door and stepped into a rush of cold air. She hurried across the platform, through another door, and into the next car.

"Might as well go down to the other end and work my way up," she decided. She began hurrying towards the other end of the long car.

Suddenly, the train lurched, and Belle went flying across the aisle. She tried to grab something to keep from falling. The luggage rack was just out of reach.

Oh, no! She fell right over the armrest of a seat and landed smack in the lap of a very fat man. The man had been sound asleep until Belle landed on him.

"Whoosh!" His breath came out in a strangled gasp. The woman next to him sat up quickly.

"Well, I never!" the woman said, and glared at Belle.

Belle tried to push herself off the fat man's lap. But it was like being caught in a big bowl

26

of pudding. Finally, the woman reached over and hit Belle on the back.

"Leave that poor man alone!" she snapped.

But the hit on her back was enough to help Belle get off the fat man's lap. She climbed out into the aisle and stood looking down at him.

"I'm—I'm—" Belle wanted to apologize, but no other words would come out. She felt so upset that she was afraid she might cry. Finally, she turned and hurried back towards her own car. When she saw Judd, she tried hard to look calm.

"How's your book?" she asked Judd, slipping into her seat beside him.

Judd looked at his book as though he had forgotten about it.

"Oh, I wasn't doing much reading," he said. "Where'd you go in such a hurry?"

The thought of telling Judd about falling into the fat man's lap was too much for Belle.

"Oh," she said, trying to sound casual. "I just wanted to stretch my legs a little."

Judd watched her for a moment. He knew there was more to it than that. But, he decided, you just never could tell about womenfolks. Best leave things alone.

Chapter 5

A Romantic Dinner

Judd could tell that Belle was upset about not being able to find her duffel bag. Since she had come back from her walk, she just sat, staring out the window.

Judd looked up as a new conductor came through the car. "First seating in the diner in ten minutes!" the conductor called.

Judd looked at Belle. Here was something to take her mind off whatever it was that bothered her. "I'm beginning to get hungry, Belle," he said. "How about you?"

Belle shook her head. "I'm not hungry," she answered.

"I thought maybe we'd go all out and eat in the dining car tonight," Judd said hopefully.

"You mean, go and order from the menu?" Belle asked. The worried look left her face for a moment.

"Sure! Why not? This is my first trip to Florida. I'd like to do things up proper," Judd said, with a grin. "Wouldn't you?"

Belle thought about the dining car. She had hoped to see it when she was hunting for her missing duffel bag. But, then, she'd had that fall. It still upset her to think about it. It was so embarrassing! But it wasn't Judd's fault she'd fallen on that fat man, she thought. And she did want them both to enjoy this trip.

"All right, Judd. I guess I *am* hungry, after all," she said, smiling.

They started off down the aisle. The dining car was two cars away. When they went past the seats where the fat man and the angry woman were sitting, Belle looked the other way.

The dining car was filling up fast. The steward showed them to a table and held the chair for Belle.

There was a linen cloth and linen napkins on the table. No paper ones like they used at home. Even the glasses were special. They were clear as crystal and stood on stems. And, in the middle of the table, there was a little vase with a pink rose in it.

Belle thought, eating at this table would *have* to be special. Just about as romantic as a dinner could be!

She took a quick look at Judd. So far, Judd hadn't said or done anything that showed he felt something special for her. Maybe sitting across such a lovely table from each other would make something happen between them.

Belle caught a glimpse of herself in the train window. What if he could read her mind? She felt herself blush and turned her head away. Then, she made herself laugh to cover up.

"It'll be fun eating in the dining car," she said in a soft voice. "How nice of you to think of it!"

Judd's face lit up with pleasure.

"Buffet service tonight, sir," their waiter said to Judd. "You and your lady can just go up to the buffet, and you'll be served whatever you want. The broiled bluefish is good tonight," he added, with a smile.

Belle liked being called Judd's "lady." She felt like she was floating as she went to the buffet. She really wanted the bluefish. But what if a fish bone got caught in her throat! She didn't want to spoil their romantic dinner.

"I'll have the chicken and biscuits, please," she told the serving man. Then, she saw some golden brown croissants in a neat serving basket. "I'd like one of those rolls, too, please," she said.

"But you're getting biscuits with the chicken," Judd reminded her.

"You'd like a croissant, ma'am?" the waiter asked. He held his hand over the basket, waiting.

"Yes, please," Belle said. "I just love croissants," she added, hoping she had said the word right.

I'll bet she never had one of those things in her whole life, Judd thought. But he didn't say anything to spoil her fun.

Belle watched as a different serving man heaped fresh salad in a pretty white bowl.

"What kind of dressing would you like, ma'am?" he asked.

"Oh, my," she said. At home, Flora always said one kind of salad dressing was enough. And, since Flora only liked Italian, they always had Italian. Belle looked at all the bottles and jars. Then, she said, "I'll have the blue cheese, please." She watched the man pour a stream of the thick, white dressing over her salad.

My, that looks good, Belle thought. I'm going to buy some blue cheese dressing at home, whether Flora likes it or not!

Then, the waiter who had shown them to their table came and picked up Belle's tray. He carried it on the tips of his fingers, way up in the air. Belle was tickled pink and hurried after him. He set down the tray and, then, held her chair. Next, he took all the dishes off the tray and placed them neatly before her. Last, he picked up her linen napkin, shook it out, and laid it across her lap. Belle heaved a big sigh of pleasure. She'd never been so waited on in her whole life!

Just then, Judd came, following another waiter. As Judd settled into his chair, a different waiter came to the table. He had a little bucket filled with ice. Nestled in the ice was a bottle of something.

The waiter picked up the bottle and wrapped a napkin around it. He gave the cork a quick twist and held the bottle out for Judd to sniff. Next, the waiter picked up one of the smaller stemmed glasses on the table and poured something into it.

"One of our nicest wines, sir," he said.

Belle couldn't believe how calm Judd was as he tasted the wine and nodded at the waiter. Just like he had wine with his dinner every night! She felt quite proud sitting across the table from him.

The waiter poured wine in her glass and filled up Judd's before he went away.

"Here's to a great trip!" Judd said. He lifted his glass of wine in a salute to Belle. Then, he drank a little and smiled at her. "This is nice," he said.

Belle agreed. She sipped her wine. It was a bit heady. But it sure did make dinner special!

They ate in happy silence, now and then looking up to smile. Belle couldn't remember ever having such a nice dinner.

"We're having dinner in Virginia, Belle," Judd said. "Leastways, I think that's where we are." He squinted out the window.

Belle leaned closer to the window and tried to see through the darkness. Then, she began to get that creepy feeling again. Slowly, she turned her head and looked around the dining car.

Right there, just a few tables away, sat that suspicious-looking man. There were two others at the table. As Belle watched, he looked up, hunting for a waiter. For a moment, he looked right into Belle's eyes. His eyes were just as black and cold as she remembered.

Belle shivered.

"Judd!" she said in a loud whisper. "There he is! He's at that table over there."

"Who is?" Judd asked, looking up.

"Why, *him!* That man!"

Judd turned quickly and looked at the table Belle had pointed out. All he saw was two people enjoying their meal.

"What's come over you, Belle?" he asked. "Looks like two people eating, to me. No call to get all excited about that."

"But there were three, Judd!" Belle said. "I saw him with my own eyes! He was right there, and now, he's not."

"All right, Belle. No need to get so excited."

"But don't you see, Judd? When he saw me looking, he left. He must know I'm onto him!"

Judd rolled his eyes and sighed. "If you say so, Belle. If you say so."

"That means my duffel bag is here on this train someplace, too. If that conductor had looked for it, I know he would have found it."

Then, she noticed the set look on Judd's face. Right away, she stopped talking. No sense making Judd upset with her. She would just bide her time.

Back in their coach seats after dinner, Belle and Judd leaned back, feeling good.

"That was lovely," Belle said. "I don't know when I've enjoyed eating my dinner more."

"'Twas nice," Judd agreed. "Sort of makes you feel like someone important. You know, just sitting there and watching the world flash by outside the train windows."

Belle smiled in agreement.

The conductor came by. He was passing out little white pillows to anybody who wanted one.

"How nice!" Belle said, taking one. "That will come in real handy," she said, thanking him. Judd took a pillow, too.

The conductor leaned over their seat. "I've got just a few light blankets, ma'am, in case you should feel chilly. If you want one later, just press that button there by the light switch."

Belle was pleased. "That's real thoughtful of you," she told him, smiling.

The conductor went on down the aisle, and Judd settled in his seat.

"Don't know about you," he said, "but that wine made me sleepy."

"We got up awfully early this morning," Belle reminded him.

"Mind if I tuck in for the night, Belle?" Judd asked.

" 'Course not. I'll do the same," Belle told him. She reached down to slip off her shoes.

Judd let down his seat back as far as it would go.

"Sure wish I had my duffel bag," Belle said. "I always brush my teeth before I go to bed!"

"Won't hurt to miss it just this once," Judd told her. "Good night, Belle."

"Good night."

Then, Judd took off his hearing aid and closed his eyes.

Chapter 6

An Accident and a Visitor

Belle wasn't really sleepy yet. She just sat, enjoying the feeling of being well fed and lazy. Judd snored beside her. Every now and then, one or two people would come wobbling down the aisle. Going to the dining car, Belle guessed. It must be nice sitting there late at night, talking, she thought. But it was nice enough just to have Judd nearby.

Now and then, a cluster of girls and boys came through the car. The girls giggled and laughed. When they almost lost their footing, they giggled even more. The boys, though, sort of swaggered. They seemed to dare the swaying car to make them fall.

They must be with that bunch that got on when we did, Belle thought. They seemed to be good kids. Nice to be young like that, she thought, smiling to herself.

Another group of boys and girls came by on their way for sodas. Just as they passed her seat, the train gave a big lurch, and one of the girls half fell into Belle's lap. Two of her friends hurried to help the girl up. The girls all giggled nervously. One of them said to Belle, "We're sorry! We didn't mean to bother you!"

Belle remembered how awful she had felt when she fell on the fat man. She smiled.

"Oh, you didn't do it on purpose. Don't fret," she told the girls. The nervous giggling stopped, and the girls smiled back at her.

Then, they were gone up the aisle, hunting for their friends.

Belle decided to go to the restroom. Bending down carefully, so she wouldn't wake Judd, Belle slipped her shoes back on. She got up and hurried along the dark, empty aisle.

There was a ladies' room at the end of their car, but the door was latched.

I'll go use the one in the next car, she thought. She started through the heavy door at the end of the car.

Once through the door, Belle felt a rush of cold air. She was between cars now. The door to the next car was across a metal platform. On one side of her was a set of heavy steel steps to the outside. Freezing air and noise came rushing up the steps. It was dark, but Belle could see a door at the bottom of the steps. The door rattled, as though it wasn't quite shut. It made her shiver to think that anyone falling down those steps could fall right off the train!

Still shivering, Belle began to hurry. The far door opened, and someone else who was in a hurry came out onto the platform. She crowded over to the side to make room for the other person, but he was coming too fast! Wham! She was knocked off her feet. She fell towards the steps, grabbing at anything to stop her fall.

Then, her hand touched the cold steel railing at the edge of the steps. She grabbed it tightly, still clutching her purse with her other hand. A shock of pain told her that she had twisted her wrist. But she had stopped her fall! She was safe! Weakly, she let herself sink onto one of the steps.

The man who had knocked her down stood frozen at the top of the steps, looking down at her. It was hard to see in the dark. But a faint light from a passing train briefly lit his face.

It was that man!

And, just as fast, he was gone.

"I musn't faint," Belle said to herself. She wanted to get up and run. But her legs felt like wet noodles, and she couldn't move. She was still clinging to the railing when someone else came by.

"Ma'am, are you all right?"

Belle took the hand that reached down to help her. Then, she looked up and saw the man's face.

It was the fat man!

"Yes. No!" she answered, feeling flustered.

"Are you all right?" he asked again.

Belle wished she could just vanish into thin air. Of all people to find her! Suddenly, she had a chilling thought. There was something going on, something scary. And she seemed to be right in the middle of it! Until she knew what it was, she wouldn't trust anyone!

She pulled herself together. "I was just careless," she said. "I was on my way to the ladies' room and must have tripped."

"I'll walk you to the restroom," the fat man said.

Before Belle could protest, he opened the door for her. He followed her back to the ladies' room in her car. It was empty now. Belle thanked him quickly and scurried inside.

Before she came out again, she listened to be sure the fat man was gone. Then, Belle hurried back to her seat.

It had been a long and exciting day. Too exciting! Her wrist hurt. And she had so much to think about. So much to try to figure out.

I'll never get to sleep now, she thought, worrying. I just know I never will.

But, in a little while, Belle dozed off.

She slept quietly until her dream started. She dreamed she was being chased by people with cold, dark eyes. Someone in the dream was pulling at her.

Or *was* it a dream?

Someone *was* tugging at her. No! They were tugging at her purse, which was wedged between her and the seat. Belle let her eyes open a tiny crack. It was hard to see but, yes, there was someone standing by her seat. She stirred, as if she were still asleep, and clutched her purse more tightly.

The tugging stopped. The figure moved silently away. Her purse was safe.

Belle opened her eyes all the way and strained to see. A man hurried up the aisle away from her. As he passed under the dim coach night-light she could see his shape clearly. It was that man!

She switched on the small overhead light and began hunting through her purse. Her wallet and traveler's checks were all there. There was a slip with the addresses and phone numbers of people friends had asked her to call while she was in Florida. And there was her return ticket, and the sheet the travel agent had given her with the name and number of the motel where they were going to stay. There was her comb, her small cosmetic bag, and some tissues. That was it. What could that man have been looking for?

Belle looked at Judd, still sound asleep. She wanted to shake him awake and tell him about all that had happened. But there wasn't anything he could do tonight. And she wanted to think about it all before she told him. She wanted to make sense out of it first.

Belle sighed and pressed the button to call the conductor.

"I'd like one of those blankets now, if I may," she said when he got there.

A few minutes later, Belle began to feel better. Somehow, having a blanket wrapped around her made her feel safer.

She settled herself to watch the lonely lights flash by outside. It wouldn't be long until morning.

Chapter 7

A Real Mystery

"Belle? Are you awake?"

Belle couldn't bring herself to open her eyes.

"Oh," she groaned, sitting up stiffly.

Then, it all came back to her in a flood. Last night, she had almost fallen off the train! Then, she was almost robbed! She had meant to think it all out. But she must have fallen asleep, because now it was morning. And Judd was wide awake, nudging her.

"Let's eat, Belle. I'm real hungry. Aren't you?" Judd asked.

Belle thought a moment. "Yep, I am," she answered, surprised at herself. "Real hungry."

"Have we got any fruit left?" asked Judd.

"Let me go wash up a bit, so's I'm awake. Then, we'll see what we have left in the line of food, Judd," Belle told him. She would wait to tell him about what happened until after they'd eaten.

"I already washed up, Belle. Want me to get the bag of food down?"

Belle nodded yes. She stood up, tugging at her skirt. She guessed it didn't look too bad for having been slept in. When Judd handed her the brown paper bag she sat back down. She set the bag on her lap and began rooting around in it.

"Darn," she said. "I thought I put the bananas right near the top." She held up two battered bananas.

Judd sighed. "Tell you what, Belle. While you go to the ladies' room to wash up, I'll go see what they've got to eat in the diner. And why don't you take the window seat for a while?"

Belle liked that idea, and hurried off to the ladies' room.

She washed her face and combed her hair. She brushed her teeth with her finger. It was better than nothing, she thought. Then, she put on a little makeup and went back to their seat.

Just as she was getting settled in the window seat, Judd appeared carrying a fairly large box. When he sat down, Belle could see that there were two plastic covered dishes in the box. And there were two cups of coffee, and two covered paper cups.

Judd looked pleased with himself. He took the cover off one plate. He handed the plate and some silverware to Belle.

"Figured with all this upset, you needed a good breakfast," he said.

Belle broke into the biggest smile he ever remembered seeing on her face.

"Blueberry pancakes and sausage! Oh, Judd, that's my favorite breakfast! How'd you know?"

"Just took a guess!" Judd said, uncovering his own plate.

For the next few minutes, they were both too busy eating to talk. Judd finally took a last swallow of coffee and set his cup down. Belle, who ate a little faster than Judd did, had been waiting for him to finish.

"Thanks so much for breakfast, Judd," Belle said, as Judd gathered up the trash.

Belle tried to think how to tell Judd about everything that had happened. Finally, she turned to him and said, "Judd, we need to talk about that man."

Judd gave a deep sigh. "I know," he said. He tried to remember what That Man looked like. Then, he laughed quietly to himself. Ever since Belle called my attention to him, I've thought of him as That Man, he thought. Not *that man,* but *That Man.* Just like it was his real name! He chuckled softly. That Belle, she sure does liven things up, he thought.

"A lot's been happening that you don't know about," Belle said.

"Such as?"

"Well, way back when we were in the train station at home, I caught That Man looking at me."

"Even if he was, there's no law against looking at people in a railroad station," Judd said. "I thought you were just being foolish."

Belle was impatient. "I know you did, Judd. But his look was, well, it was so cold. It gave me goose bumps."

"All right. What else happened?"

As calmly as she could, Belle told Judd about That Man watching her in the dining car. Then, she told him about being pushed in the passage between the two railway cars.

"You mean, he made you fall?" Judd said, in an angry voice. Then, he looked at Belle with worry on his face. "Are you all right now? Why didn't you wake me up and tell me last night?"

"I'm all right now, Judd. A little stiff, maybe, but that hot coffee sure helped. And I didn't wake you up last night because I wanted to think about it. Anyway, you didn't have your hearing aid on."

Judd looked a little sheepish. "I can't sleep with that thing in my ear," he said.

Belle nodded. Then, she told him about her dream and finding That Man trying to steal her purse.

"And I never knew a thing," Judd said, disgusted. "Why did he want your purse?"

"I don't know," Belle said. "It just doesn't make sense."

"Let's go back over everything," Judd said. "First, you saw That Man looking at you in the train station. Then, your bag got mixed up with somebody else's. And you say it was That Man who took yours. Then, he knocked you down. Then, he tried to get your purse."

Judd stopped to think a minute. "What's in your purse and your duffel bag that he wants, Belle? It doesn't make sense. But it sure looks like there's *something* going on."

"That's what I think, too," Belle agreed.

They sat for a few moments, thinking.

"Well, what do you think we should do, Belle?" Judd asked, at last.

"I think the first thing is to find my duffel bag. I know it's somewhere here on the train."

"If we find where That Man is sitting, we'll find your bag!" said Judd, sounding excited.

"Right!" said Belle. Then, she remembered the fat man. She sure didn't want to run into him again. "Why don't you take the cars ahead, Judd? I'll check the ones going back."

"Sounds good to me," Judd agreed.

Belle hurried back to the car behind theirs, and Judd got busy looking at the luggage racks.

In the next car, Belle found a lot of empty seats. Everybody must be up at the diner, she thought. It made hunting for her bag easier. She acted casual, as though she were just up for a walk. But she kept looking for That Man.

Just like Sherlock Holmes! she thought.

Belle went from car to car. But she couldn't find him. He wasn't in any of the coaches. When she got to the sleeping cars she was stumped. The doors to the sleepers were locked. She'd just have to pass up the sleepers.

And that's probably just where That Man is! she thought, upset.

She went on through the sleeper cars and found more coach cars. Carefully, she looked at all the racks. Finally, she reached the front of the train, with no sign of That Man. Belle turned back. She hoped Judd was having better luck.

Back in their car, she found Judd waiting.

"I didn't see a sign of him. Did you?" Judd said.

"No." She shook her head sadly.

Judd felt bad. He had wanted very much to find That Man. He knew it would really have pleased Belle. She looked so let down.

"It's a real mystery," she said.

Judd agreed.

After they had sat for a few minutes, Belle spoke. "You know, That Man must be in a sleeper. It's the only place he could be that we wouldn't see him."

"So, now what do we do?" Judd asked.

"I'll think of something!" she said.

Judd looked at Belle for a moment. By darn, she will, too! he thought, smiling.

Chapter 8

Florida at Last!

There wasn't time to think about That Man after that. The conductor said the train would get to Jacksonville in about 20 minutes. He took the name of the motel where Belle and Judd would be staying.

"Somebody from the railroad will call you early tonight about your bag, ma'am," the conductor said. "I'll just take that other bag now."

"I'm not letting go of this bag until I get mine back," Belle said, clutching the bag tightly.

"Well, ma'am, if you feel that way—"

"You bet I do," Belle said.

"OK, Belle," Judd said. "C'mon now. Everything's ready to go."

Everybody else seemed in a hurry to get off the train, too. Judd and Belle crowded into the aisle with the other passengers.

"Doesn't seem possible we've been on this train over twenty hours, does it, Judd?" Belle asked, taking a quick look at their luggage.

"Seems longer than that to me," Judd said. "I didn't get a wink of sleep last night!"

Belle started to say that she had heard him snore. She stopped herself just in time. No sense hurting his feelings. Instead, she just smiled and said, "We both need a good night's sleep."

Judd smiled in agreement. "You're sure you reserved us a car at the car rental place, Belle?" he asked.

"Of course, I am. You don't think I'd forget a thing like that, do you?"

"No, I guess not. It's just—well, to tell the truth, I'm nervous." Judd looked out the window. "There's Jacksonville," he said, pointing.

Belle looked at Judd and saw that his cheeks were a bit flushed.

"Are you nervous because you'll be seeing your son soon, Judd?" she asked gently.

Judd nodded. "It just occurred to me that I've never met his wife, and now here they are with two children!"

With a screech and shudder, the train finally stopped.

"Move ahead, Judd," Belle said. The conductor had just opened the doors to the train station platform, and people began pushing.

For the next few minutes, it was all Belle could do to hang onto her two bags and her purse. She tried to keep up with Judd.

"Need help, Belle?" he asked.

"No, thanks. I'm doing fine," she answered, as they both finally got through the doorway. Once out on the station platform, people began hurrying away.

"Whoosh!" said Belle. "Everybody sure is in a hurry."

"Can't stop now, Belle," Judd said. "There's only one bus that can take us to the car rental place, and I see it loading up."

Belle looked where Judd was pointing. She grabbed her two bags and hurried after him towards the little bus.

"Bus to Easy Car Rental," a man standing by the bus called out. "You folks going to Easy?"

Belle nodded, and the driver took her bags. The driver loaded the bags while Belle and Judd found seats. A few other people came, and then the driver got in. He pulled out a long, white paper and checked off their names.

"Guess that's everybody," he said. Then, he started the bus and headed out onto the highway.

In a few minutes, the bus pulled off the highway and onto a narrow street. The bus passed several car rental places before it pulled up in front of Easy Car Rental.

"Here we are, folks," the bus driver said. "Go inside, and the girl at the desk will help you get your cars." He got out and started unloading the luggage.

"Well," Belle said with a sigh. "I'm beginning to feel like we're finally in Florida."

Judd grinned at her as they went inside the office.

Not long after, a cheery young woman showed them where to sign their names and gave them keys to their car. "Have fun, folks!" she said, as they left the office.

Judd found their car in the parking space where the young woman had said it would be.

"My, my, my!" he said. "Just look at that car, Belle. Brand new!" He walked all around the blue car, admiring it. "I've never driven such a new car before!"

Judd threw his sweater in the back seat and loaded their luggage. Belle climbed into the passenger seat. She really wanted to drive the new car, too. But, she figured, let Judd have the first chance. I'll get to drive it soon enough.

Chapter 9

That Man Again

The woman in the office had given them a map showing how to get to Florida Beach. Judd opened it, while Belle looked around.

For a moment, a familiar figure caught her eye in the car rental place next door.

"Judd! Did you see who that was?" Belle cried, grabbing his arm. "It's That Man! He's here in Jacksonville, and he's rented a car, too!"

Judd looked to where she pointed, but he didn't see anyone. "Are you sure, Belle?" he asked.

Belle swung her head to look at Judd. Her eyes were shooting sparks. "Of course, I'm sure!" she said. "I may be getting older, but my eyes haven't given out yet!"

"OK, OK!" Judd said quickly. "I didn't mean to say you were wrong. I'd sort of forgotten about That Man. What with this dandy new car and going to meet my son and all."

Belle smiled. "I know," she said. She settled back in her seat. "Well, what are we waiting for? Let's get started!"

Judd laughed and started the car. Then, he headed out onto the road.

"You take the map, Belle, and be the navigator," he said. "I'll be the pilot for now."

In no time, they were headed south.

"Watch for Route 10, Judd," Belle said, studying the map. "We take Route 10 all the way to Tallahassee. Then, we take the Pensacola turnoff onto Route 20. We keep following the signs for Pensacola until we get to Panama City. Then, we watch for signs to Florida Beach."

"How far is it?" Judd asked.

Belle got out a pencil and started adding up the little numbers on the map. Finally, she said, "It's about three hundred twenty-five miles or so, Judd. Though, to be truthful, I've never been one whit of good with numbers!"

"That's OK," Judd said, laughing happily. "The way I feel now, with this new car under me, I don't care how far it is."

"Oh, watch it! There's a sign for Route 10!"

"I see it," Judd said, working his way neatly through the traffic.

"Well, now," he said, as the car eased onto a big express highway. "This will be a cinch. We'll be at the Pensacola turnoff in no time."

"Well, it'll be at least six hours, won't it?"

"Guess about that. Why?" Judd asked.

"That's too long to wait to eat," Belle said. "I think, after we drive about halfway, we should look for a nice place to stop and have a meal."

"Sounds good to me," Judd agreed.

The car was running smoothly, and the road was easy to follow. Belle had time to think back to seeing That Man again.

"Where do you think he's going?" she asked.

"Who?" asked Judd.

"Why, That Man, of course!" she said.

"Belle, did it ever occur to you that he just came to Florida for a nice vacation?"

"Oh, pooh!" Belle snapped. "He's been acting too suspicious to just be on vacation."

"You think he's following us?" Judd asked. He looked quickly at Belle. She sure did look serious. He snorted. "Oh, for Pete's sake, Belle. What would he want to be following *us* for?"

"I don't know, Judd, but I think he is!" She had been looking out the back window. Now, she turned and put her hand on Judd's arm. "He's back there, Judd. I just know he is!"

Judd didn't say anything.

Belle turned around in her seat and looked out the back window.

A moment later, she shouted, "There he is, Judd! That's him, driving that little green car!"

"But, Belle," Judd said, sighing. "There are so many cars on the road! You can't be sure."

"Don't believe me if you don't want to, Judd Hagadorn," Belle said.

She sounded so sure, Judd thought he'd better listen to her.

"Well," he said slowly, "you could be right, I guess. But, try to relax and enjoy the ride, anyway."

Belle sighed. "I wish I could forget about him. But I won't feel right till I get my own bag back."

"There isn't a blessed thing you can do about him or your duffel bag right now," Judd said. "The conductor promised you'd hear about your duffel bag real soon. Meanwhile, look at how fresh and green everything is. Looks a lot better to me than that dirty old snow we left up in New York!"

"You're right, Judd," Belle said, sighing. "I'm letting That Man spoil things for me. That's stupid. I'm not going to do that anymore."

They drove along in pleasant silence for a few more miles. Then, Belle opened up the map again.

"I guess Tallahassee would be a good place to get some lunch," she said. She looked up from the map to see what Judd thought of her idea.

"How far is it?" he asked.

"About, about—oh, darn!" Belle said. "You would ask. Well, it's about two inches on the map," she finally said.

"I don't want to know in inches, Belle. I want to know how many miles!" Judd said.

Belle squinted at the map. "Best I can tell, it's about seventy miles." She paused. "Or eighty."

"It doesn't matter, Belle," Judd said. "I'm hungry now. If we see a nice place on this side of Tallahassee, let's stop."

Belle agreed. She took one more look out the back window. No green cars in sight. Relieved, she folded up the map and went back to watching the Florida landscape.

Belle had just about forgotten That Man by the time Judd found a place for lunch.

"I wonder if they serve grits here," she said.

"Grits? You really want grits?" Judd asked.

"Sure do," Belle answered. "Haven't had good, southern grits since I was a child. They used to make them with some kind of gravy.

Let's see, um, I think it was a color. Oh, I know," she said happily. "It was redeye gravy!"

"Redeye gravy?" said Judd. "Sounds awful."

"Oh, it's not made from red eyes, silly. It's made from ham. You know how that little ham bone looks like an eye?"

"You mean, they make ham gravy for the grits?" Judd asked.

"Yes," Belle answered, a bit smug.

"Then why don't they just call it ham gravy? Why do they have to call it redeye gravy?"

"Oh, Judd," said Belle, laughing. "Just park the car so we can go get some lunch." She looked at the little restaurant Judd had picked out. "I'll bet they have good home cooking here."

Belle and Judd found a seat near the window. They spent a delicious time reading the menu.

"Hot buttermilk biscuits, honey-baked chicken, and a fresh garden salad," Judd ordered.

"I'd like some ham and grits," Belle said. She ordered a salad, too.

In a few minutes, the heaped plates were set in front of them. Judd broke open one of the biscuits.

"Looks like we picked the right place to eat, Belle," he said. "Never saw a lighter biscuit in my life." He spread the biscuit with butter and drizzled honey all over it. Then, he ate the whole thing and licked the honey off his fingers. "Now, that's eating!" he said.

Belle enjoyed her ham and grits, too. The meal brought back memories of a happy time she had spent in Florida with her family.

"Don't know what you see so special in that stuff," Judd said, motioning towards the grits.

But, before he got to finish what he was saying, Belle let out a yell. She jumped up from the table and raced across the room. In no time, she was out the door. Judd could see her running across the parking lot towards their car.

"Oh, my gosh!" he yelled. Someone was breaking into their car! He ran after Belle as fast as he could.

But Belle hadn't been fast enough. A car zoomed out of the parking lot just as she got there. Judd was right behind her.

"Oh, damn. It was That Man!" Belle said, climbing into their car angrily.

Judd knew she was really upset. He had never heard her swear before.

"Look where he broke the lock, Belle! Did he get anything?" Judd peered into the back seat.

"I don't know!" she said as she burrowed into the things piled in their car. Then, she

climbed back out of the car and stood there, looking angry.

"He took the other duffel bag!" she said, stamping her foot. "Now, he has them both!"

"We'd better call the police," Judd said.

"And tell them what?" Belle asked. "The railroad people already know about my duffel bag. Not a very expensive bag, anyway. And all it's got in it are my shoes and toothbrush and things. Now, we're going to tell the police that the man came and stole his *own* bag back?"

Judd looked at Belle a moment, and then nodded. "You're right."

"Judd," Belle said, sounding like her mind was made up. "I think we're just going to have to try to catch up with That Man and find out what's going on."

Judd thought that was crazy. But what else could they do?

"I think you may be right, Belle," he said.

"Then let's get started!" Belle said.

"First, I've gotta go back and pay for our lunch," Judd said. "Then, we'll get right back on the highway."

Judd went into the restaurant. Soon, he came running back and got behind the wheel. With a screech, he swung the car back onto the highway.

"Next stop's the Pensacola turnoff," he said. "Unless we catch up to that green car first!"

Judd drove like he was going to a fire. Belle had never ridden in a car going so fast. At least, not that she could remember. She made sure her seat belt was good and snug.

Watching Judd drive, Belle could see how serious he had gotten about this whole thing. Somehow, it made him look younger than she'd ever seen him.

Belle was bouncing around on her seat like a rag doll. Since That Man had come into her life, things had sure been lively! She tried to sort it all out. That Man may have tried to hurt her on the train. And he'd tried to take her purse when she was sleeping. And, now, there was this strange business of breaking into their car and having both duffel bags!

She sneaked a quick look at Judd's face. Maybe she should be scared, but she wasn't. Instead, it was exciting! She felt just as if she were in the middle of a TV detective show!

Chapter 10

The Search

"I don't know why we haven't seen that green car yet," Belle said.

"Thought sure we'd catch up to him by now," Judd said.

"That last sign said it's only fifteen miles to the Pensacola turnoff. What if That Man isn't going our way, Judd?"

"Well, we'll deal with that when we have to," Judd answered. "Meanwhile, watch for that turnoff sign, so we don't miss it."

They drove pell-mell down the road. Judd didn't slow his pace a bit. So, when Belle finally cried, "There it is! The Pensacola turnoff!" Judd had to stamp on the brake.

"Whoosh!" Belle's breath came out in a big sigh as she was pressed against her seatbelt.

"Sorry, Belle, I sort of forgot how fast I was going," Judd said. "I didn't mean to slam you around like that!"

"I'm all right," Belle told him. "But now that we've turned off, the road is narrower. So, maybe you'd better not drive so fast."

"To tell the truth," Judd said, "I'd be afraid to drive that fast on this road. Anyway, we don't want to miss that green car! He might have pulled off somewhere."

They followed the signs for Pensacola. After a while, they started seeing clumps of buildings. They were entering Panama City.

"Looks like a bigger town than I thought," Belle said. "It's kind of pretty, too, don't you think?"

There were bushes everywhere, just covered with blossoms.

"Wow!" said Judd, pointing. "Look at that! I never saw such a big palm tree!"

"Ha!" said Belle. "When did you ever see *any* palm trees before we came to Florida?"

Judd laughed. "You're right, Belle. I'm no expert on palm trees. That one was sure a granddaddy, though!"

They almost missed seeing the green car.

"Over there! Look over there, Judd!" Belle cried. She sounded excited. "There's a green car that looks like the one That Man was driving!"

Judd turned the steering wheel to the right and slammed on the brakes, all at once.

"Where?" he blurted.

Belle pointed. There, in front of a little cafe, was a green car.

"I see a car, Belle. But are you sure it's green?"

"Oh, you and your colors!" Belle laughed in spite of herself. "Pull in there, Judd. I want to look at it closer."

Judd backed up and pulled into the parking lot near the green car.

"How are we going to find out if that's the right one?" Judd asked. "If it isn't, we might get in trouble for trespassing or something."

"Oh, pooh!" Belle snorted. "We've come too far to back out now, Judd!" She started to climb out of the car.

"Hold your horses, Belle!" Judd said, reaching over to stop her. "Let's do this thing right, if we're gonna do it." He thought a moment. "I think I ought to be the one to go look at the car. After all, there's no sense you taking chances."

"You mean, because I'm a woman?" Belle said, with fire in her eyes.

"No, no, Belle. Not at all—" His words died out. "I just mean, well, I'd like to go and look!"

"He took *my* duffel bag, Judd Hagadorn," Belle said. "I think that gives me the right to go look at that car."

Judd sighed. He knew when to back down.

"OK, Belle. But please be careful!" he said.

Judd pulled his hand away from her arm, and Belle got out of the car. She looked around to see that nobody was watching. Then, she bent down to the open window.

"Here I go, Judd. Wish me luck!"

Belle strolled slowly towards the green car. She stopped and picked a blossom off a red azalea bush and pretended to be admiring it. Then, she started walking again.

She's trying to act like she just happens to be there, Judd thought. But if I was That Man, she wouldn't fool me for a minute!

Slowly and carefully, Belle walked towards the green car. When she was almost there, she turned and gave a funny little wave to Judd.

She must want me to know she's OK, he thought. Well, I can *see* that, for Pete's sake! Wish she'd hurry up and get this over with!

Belle finally reached the car. She peeped in the driver's window, as though she were admiring it. She shook her head to say that the car was empty.

Then, she sort of inched her way back to the trunk. She put her hand on the edge of the trunk lid, and looked all around. There wasn't anyone around.

Judd began to sweat. He had a bad feeling about this, somehow. Why hadn't they just gone to the police?

Just then, That Man came out of the cafe. He was carrying a duffel bag and looking pleased with himself.

Belle let out a yell and started running towards That Man. She grabbed the duffel bag from him and turned back towards their car. Before she could run away, That Man grabbed her arms and began tugging at the duffel bag.

Judd jumped out of the car to run and help her. But, before Judd could reach Belle, That Man dragged her into his car, and started driving away!

The green car zoomed across the parking lot, tires screeching. Judd could see that Belle was fighting back, though. She wasn't going meekly!

The last Judd saw of Belle, she was in the front seat of That Man's car. She was using the duffel bag to bash That Man on the head over and over again!

Before Judd got back to his car, the green car had dashed around a corner, and was gone.

Chapter 11

Kidnapped!

For a moment, Judd sat in the car, stunned. Belle had been kidnapped!

Then, he roared into action. He stomped on the gas pedal as hard as he could. Stones sprayed out all over the parking lot. He drove out of the parking lot and took off in the direction the other car had taken. He leaned over the steering wheel as though he could force the car to go even faster.

But, soon, it was clear that That Man had gotten away.

Judd saw a police car parked near a corner. He pulled right up next to it and stopped.

The policeman opened his mouth to yell at Judd for his driving. But, before he could say a word, Judd leaned across the seat and yelled, "A man just kidnapped my friend!"

The policeman's mouth fell open.

"Call for help!" Judd yelled. "Right now!"

"OK, OK. Just stop yelling and tell me what happened." The policeman leaned out his open window.

As fast as he could, Judd told him the whole story.

"Don't go away," the officer said. Then, he rolled up his window and started speaking into his car phone. He kept looking through the glass at Judd, then back at some kind of a list he had.

After what seemed like forever to Judd, the policeman rolled down his window again.

"Follow me!" the policeman snapped. Then, he started the patrol car, turned on the siren, and started racing through town.

Judd had to go through a red light to keep up with the police car. He just crossed his fingers and kept driving.

They finally stopped in front of a big cement building. The policeman got out of his car and motioned for Judd to get out, too. Judd followed the policeman inside.

This was Judd's first time in a big police station. But there was no time to look around.

The policeman introduced Judd to the captain. The captain listened carefully to Judd's story. He asked Judd to describe That Man. Halfway through the story, he started nodding his head.

When Judd finished telling everything he could, he sat back in his chair. He suddenly felt awfully tired.

"Do you think you can find her?" Judd asked. He had thought there would be a lot of policemen running around and carrying guns, like on TV. Instead, the captain just dialed a number on his phone and spoke very fast into it.

When the captain hung up, Judd couldn't be quiet any longer. "Aren't you going to do anything?" he asked. "My friend is in trouble!"

The captain smiled briefly. "Something *is* being done, sir," he said. "My men have been waiting for this break for a long time."

71

Judd didn't know what to say.

"Just sit tight," the captain told him. "You've already been a big help."

"What do you mean? What about Belle?"

"We'll fill you in on the whole story, just as soon as my men call back. Meanwhile, there's a phone you can use if you need to call anyone."

"Call anyone? In Panama City?" Judd just sat looking at the captain. Then, it hit him. His son, Ralph, lived in Florida Beach, just outside Panama City. And Ralph and his wife were expecting Judd and Belle! Judd looked at his watch. "Oh, bullets!" he said out loud.

The captain looked at him.

"My son's been expecting me to call him all day," Judd explained. "I guess I'd better use that phone."

Judd got hold of his son, Ralph, and explained what had happened. Ralph wanted to know if there was anything he could do to help. Judd said no.

"You're sure you don't want me to come over there and be with you?" Ralph asked.

"No thanks, Ralph. No sense both of us just sitting here waiting. I wouldn't be much company right now, anyway. I'm too worried about Belle."

"Well, all right. Call as soon as you know anything. I'll stay right here by the phone."

Judd hung up feeling that it was nice to have his son nearby.

When the phone rang, the captain grabbed the receiver and listened for a few seconds. Then, he slammed the phone down and jumped up. He looked at Judd.

"They've spotted a green car over on First Street that's moving too fast," the captain said in a clipped voice. "They've got a tail on it. Want to come with me?"

Judd nodded and got up, hurrying out the door after the captain. All he could think about was Belle. He didn't want That Man to hurt her.

The patrol car went rocketing along, with its sirens wailing. Judd was tempted to turn off his hearing aid, but he didn't want to miss anything.

It seemed forever before Judd saw flashing lights and other police cars coming towards them. Then, their car screeched to a stop right behind another car with flashing lights. When Judd climbed out of the car, he saw that they had blocked the street. There was a car caught between the patrol cars. The police had That Man blocked so he couldn't get away!

Chapter 12

A Real, Live Hero

Judd rushed towards That Man's car. That Man was standing in the street on the driver's side. He had his legs spread apart and his hands on the side of the car. His clothes were all torn, and his forehead was bleeding from a long scratch. He looked awful. Two policemen were talking to him. They were both holding guns on him.

"Just keep that woman off me!" That Man said, glaring at the passenger side of the car.

Judd hurried to the passenger side. The door was wide open, and there was Belle! She looked terrible. Her clothes were ripped, and her long hair had come out of the bun she always wore it in. It was all loose and flying in every direction. But she was alive!

"Are you all right, Belle?" Judd asked.

Belle laughed a funny kind of laugh. "I guess so, Judd. I'm not real sure yet!"

She started to get up, but one of the policemen stopped her.

"Just sit right there, ma'am, until the doctor comes to check you over. You never can tell, when something like this happens. People get hurt, but they're so keyed up they don't really notice it."

Belle settled back in the seat. Judd tried to think of something to say, but the words all got stuck in his throat.

"Look, Judd," Belle said. "I got my duffel bag back!" She rummaged around and held up her blue duffel bag.

"I'll take the other one, now, ma'am," the policeman said.

Belle handed him the green duffel bag. It was torn in two places and looked like a truck had run over it. Judd remembered seeing Belle hit That Man over the head with it. He smiled in spite of himself.

"The captain will want to see this right off," the policeman said.

"But why?" Judd asked.

"Wait'll you hear!" Belle said. "I can't believe this all happened!"

"What are you talking about?" Judd demanded.

But, just then, the doctor arrived in a mobile unit, and someone brought him over to Belle. He talked to Belle for a few minutes. Then, he started to take her to the mobile unit.

The captain walked over just as Judd started to object.

"It's OK," the captain told him. "The doctor just wants to examine your friend." He looked at Judd as though he knew how Judd was feeling. That was funny, because Judd didn't even know how he was feeling! All he knew was that he was awfully tired, and his stomach hurt. He had been so worried about Belle.

It wasn't long before Belle and the doctor came back out of the mobile unit. The doctor had given her a piece of tape to hold her torn blouse together.

The captain and Judd helped her into their car.

"You go home and get a good night's sleep now," the captain said. "Call me at this number as soon as you can in the morning." He handed Belle a little white card with his name and phone number on it. "I'll send a car to pick you up."

Judd listened, amazed.

The captain turned to him. "Mr. Hagadorn, I want to thank you for your help. And your friend here, well, I don't know many women with her courage. Kidnapped and in a strange car, and she fought him like a wildcat! You can really be proud of her!"

He smiled at both of them, shaking his head. "You two did us a real service today."

"We did?" Judd asked.

"Yep. That man was Willy Williams. For a long time we've known that he was fencing hot jewels. He'd pick them up somewhere in the Northeast. Then, he'd bring them down here to Florida. We've kept a pretty close watch on him. But we could never catch him with the goods.

"But, this time, Williams made a mistake. He must have spotted our agent in the New York station. So, he picked your duffel bag to switch with, in case the agent got too close. I guess he saw that your blue bag looked almost like his, and he didn't figure you'd notice right away. But, once he'd switched bags, he had to find out where you'd be staying in Florida, so he could get his bag back. My guess is he planned on coming to your motel and pulling a big act. You know, saying how sorry he was to get the wrong bag and all that."

"But what was so special about his bag?" Judd asked.

"Stolen jewels, Judd!" Belle broke in. "In a false bottom! That's why he tried to get my purse. He was looking for motel reservations or something, so he could find us later."

"You had his bag with the stolen jewels, Belle?"

"Enough jewels to nail him for a long time," the captain said, smiling. "Once you told us about how he'd taken your friend's bag, we could pretty well guess what he was up to."

"You mean, he was coming here to sell the jewels?" Judd asked. "But, I thought it was Miami where all that bad stuff went on."

"Williams was smart. Sometimes, he sold the stuff in Miami. Sometimes, he worked with a guy who has a fishing boat. They'd take the stuff from Pensacola to a private dock near New Orleans and sell it there.

"But he didn't figure on you, ma'am," the captain said, laughing.

"Are the jewels still in the bag?" Judd asked.

The captain nodded. "You can see them when you come down to the station tomorrow. Right now, they're getting tagged for use as evidence."

Judd and Belle listened, hardly believing they were really mixed up in all this.

"Oh, and you'll get to meet the agent who was on the train," the captain told them.

"An agent? On our train?" Judd said.

"Yep," said the captain. "You might even have seen him. He's a great, big fat man."

Neither Judd nor the captain could figure out why Belle suddenly started to choke.

"Are you all right?" the captain asked.

"Yes. Oh, yes," Belle told him. Silently, she wondered if she would ever get away from that fat man.

"OK, then," the captain said. "Well, you might as well be on your way to your son's now. I know he'll be waiting."

Judd climbed into the car beside Belle. He looked at her for a moment before he turned on the motor.

"Oh, don't look at me, Judd," she said. "And, for heaven's sake, don't take me to meet your son's family looking the way I do!" She was near tears. "I wanted to make such a good impression. And, now, it's all spoiled!"

Judd drove the car a little way down the road. When they came to a quiet place shaded by a big tree, he stopped. He turned off the motor. Then, he turned to look at Belle.

"Belle," he began. "I'm not much good at this sort of thing. But, you're a real hero to me. And I think you look just beautiful!"

Then, he leaned over and kissed her.

Belle just sat there as Judd started the car. She watched him drive. A small smile started in the corners of her mouth and didn't stop until it had lit up her whole face.

And to think, she thought, I've got him for all the rest of this week. And the long trip home on the train, too!

Belle inched a little closer to Judd and leaned her head on his shoulder. Then, she closed her eyes and sighed.

She went right on smiling.